THE HISTORY OF THE BUFFALO BILLS

THE HISTORY OF THE

BUFFALO

Published by Creative Education

123 South Broad Street

Mankato, Minnesota 56001

Creative Education is an imprint of The Creative Company.

DESIGN AND PRODUCTION BY **EVANSDAY DESIGN**

Copyright © 2005 Creative Education.

International copyright reserved in all countries.

No part of this book may be reproduced in any form

without written permission from the publisher.

Printed in the United States of America

LIBRARY OF CONGRESS CATALOGING-IN-PUBLICATION DATA

Nichols, John, 1966–

The history of the Buffalo Bills / by John Nichols.

p. cm. — (NFL today)

Summary: Highlights the key personalities and memorable games in the history

of the football team that made it to the Super Bowl four straight years in

the early 1990s.

ISBN 1-58341-289-1

1. Buffalo Bills (Football team)—History—Juvenile literature. [1. Buffalo Bills

(Football team)—History. 2. Football—History.] I. Title. II. Series.

GV956.B83N55 2004

796.332'64'0974797—dc22   2003063098

First edition

9 8 7 6 5 4 3 2 1

COVER PHOTO: linebacker Takeo Spikes

PHOTOGRAPHS BY

AP/Wide World Photos, Corbis (Bettmann), Getty Images, Icon Sports Media Inc., SportsChrome USA

THE CITY OF **BUFFALO** IS LOCATED IN THE NORTHWEST CORNER OF NEW YORK, ON THE SHORES OF LAKE ERIE. BUFFALO IS KNOWN AS A GATEWAY TO THE MAJESTIC WATERS OF NEARBY NIAGARA FALLS AND AS A RESULT IS A POPULAR DESTINATION FOR HONEYMOONERS AND VACATIONERS. THE CITY IS FAMOUS TOO FOR ITS POWERFUL WINTER STORMS, WHICH HAVE BEEN KNOWN TO DUMP SEVERAL FEET OF SNOW IN JUST A FEW SHORT HOURS. BUFFALO IS ALSO A CITY THAT LOVES SPORTS. SINCE 1960, PROFESSIONAL FOOTBALL HAS HELD A SPECIAL PLACE IN THE HEARTS OF THE CITY'S CITIZENS. THAT YEAR, BUFFALO WELCOMED A TEAM IN THE NEW AMERICAN FOOTBALL LEAGUE (AFL). THE CLUB WAS NAMED THE BUFFALO BILLS AFTER COLORFUL WILD WEST HUNTER AND ENTERTAINER "BUFFALO" BILL CODY, AND LIKE ITS NAMESAKE, THE BILLS FRANCHISE WAS SOON ENTERTAINING FANS WITH SOME GREAT SHOWS.

[Running back Joe Cribbs]

IN THE 1940S, a team called the Buffalo Bills was formed as part of a pro league called the All-American Football Conference (AAFC). In 1950, the AAFC merged with the National Football League (NFL). Three AAFC teams were absorbed into the NFL. Four teams, including Buffalo, were not.

A few years later, Lamar Hunt, a wealthy Texas businessman, asked the NFL to let him start a new team. When the league turned him down, Hunt contacted seven wealthy friends. Together, they decided to start their own league—the AFL—in 1959. Many people thought the eight men were crazy to compete against the mighty NFL for fans. The move was considered so brash that sportswriters referred to the prospective AFL owners as the "Foolish Club."

One of the first Buffalo stars, 250-pound fullback Cookie Gilchrist was famous for his power.

Quick and strong-armed quarterback Jack Kemp was named the AFL's Player of the Year in 1965

One of the club members was millionaire businessman Ralph Wilson. A Michigan native, Wilson
chose Buffalo as the home for his new team. Under
his guidance, the Buffalo Bills were reborn in 1960.
The Bills were not a winning team early on, but
the great efforts of such players as big running
back Wray Carlton made the team a hit with the
region's football-hungry fans.

The Bills finally started winning in 1963. By then
the team had a core of stars that included quarterbacks Jack Kemp and Daryle Lamonica, burly
fullback Cookie Gilchrist, and sure-handed receiver
Elbert Dubenion. Led by fiery coach Lou Saban, the
Bills made the playoffs in 1963 and then captured
the AFL title in 1964 by defeating the San Diego
Chargers 20–7. "The city accepted us and support-
ed us when we were down," said Carlton. "It feels
great to give them a championship."

In 1965, the Bills met the Chargers in the AFL
championship game again. This time a Kemp
touchdown pass and three field goals from kicker
Pete Gogolak led to a 23–0 Buffalo victory. Before
the 1966 season, Saban left town. Gilchrist and
Lamonica had both been traded as well, and Buffalo
began to fade. By the end of the decade, the once-
proud Bills were back where they began—a strug-
gling franchise looking for answers.

IN 1970, THE AFL and NFL merged, with the 10 former AFL teams joining three established NFL franchises to form the American Football Conference (AFC). Looking for a fresh start in the new league, Buffalo decided to build around running back O.J. Simpson. Nicknamed "the Juice," Simpson had won the Heisman Trophy as college football's best player in 1968, and the Bills had selected him with the top overall pick in the 1969 NFL Draft. Yet despite his talent, Simpson—and the Bills—struggled in his first few seasons in Buffalo.

By the end of the 1971 season, a frustrated Simpson considered quitting. Luckily for the Bills, Lou Saban then returned as head coach and made clear his plans to revive the team. Handing the ball to Simpson during practice, the coach said to his offensive linemen, "There's your meal ticket. Go block for him."

In his two stints as Bills head coach, Lou Saban posted seven winning records in nine total seasons

The Bills linemen did block for Simpson. Joe DeLamielleure, Reggie McKenzie, and Dave Foley grew so skilled at opening holes that they became known as the "Electric Company," in charge of turning on the Juice. Simpson ran for 1,251 yards in 1972 and followed it up with an NFL-record 2,003 yards in 1973. "O.J. was a thing of beauty to watch," said Bills cornerback Robert James. "He did things that nobody had seen before on a football field."

Simpson's resurgence, along with solid contributions from quarterback Joe Ferguson and receivers J.D. Hill and Ahmad Rashad, vaulted the Bills back into contention. Unfortunately, the good Buffalo teams of the mid-1970s continually ran into the great AFC teams of that era: the Pittsburgh Steelers and Miami Dolphins. Constantly thwarted by their two main conference rivals, the Bills began to falter. A 2–12 season led to Saban's departure in 1976, and a knee injury to Simpson in 1977 ended his career in Buffalo. The Juice would play two final seasons for the San Francisco 49ers before retiring in 1979.

REBUILDING WITH "GROUND CHUCK">

IN 1978, THE Bills hired former Los Angeles Rams coach
Chuck Knox to lead the team. While with the Rams, Knox
had earned a reputation as a believer in old-fashioned
football—a coach who wanted a powerful defense paired
with a steady, conservative offense. The Bills struggled
at first under Knox, but by 1980, the man nicknamed
"Ground Chuck" (because of his love for running-based
offenses) had Buffalo ready to compete.

Buffalo put together some strong seasons in the early 1980s under head coach Chuck Knox

Powerful end Bruce Smith (left) arrived in Buffalo in 1985 and quickly became the heart of the defense^

Coach Knox's rugged defense was anchored by nose tackle Fred Smerlas and featured linebackers Isiah Robertson and Phil Villapiano. The rushing attack, meanwhile, was led by Joe Cribbs. When Cribbs entered the league in 1980 at 5-foot-11 and 190 pounds, many people thought he was too small to be an effective NFL back. But the young running back quickly proved otherwise, rushing for more than 1,000 yards in three of his first four seasons. "What they didn't measure on Joe was his toughness," noted Smerlas. "Pound for pound, Joe was the toughest guy in the league."

Knox's team made the playoffs in 1980 and 1981 but was knocked out each time, first by the San Diego Chargers, then by the Cincinnati Bengals. Even with those postseason defeats, Bills fans were confident that their team was on the rise. But the dream was shattered by a strike-shortened 1982 season and the departure of Cribbs and Knox. By 1986, the Bills had stumbled to three straight losing seasons and were again looking for a savior.

MIDWAY THROUGH A dismal 1986 season, the Bills brought in Marv Levy as their new head coach. Levy was known for his great intelligence and never-ending enthusiasm for the game, and his optimism was a breath of fresh air for the downtrodden Bills. In 1987, Buffalo began to turn the corner, posting a 7–8 record. By the end of the 1989 season, the Bills had captured two straight AFC Eastern Division titles and were a young team on the rise. "When we were down, Marv showed us the way up," said receiver Steve Tasker.

Steve Tasker was a fearless player who specialized in returning kicks and tackling on kickoffs.

Versatile halfback Thurman Thomas rushed for more than 1,000 yards in eight straight seasons^

Jim Kelly threw 237 touchdown passes for the Bills^

Levy rebuilt the Bills around four special players: defensive end Bruce Smith, receiver Andre Reed, quarterback Jim Kelly, and running back Thurman Thomas. Smith and Reed both came to Buffalo in the 1985 NFL Draft but from very different backgrounds. Smith was a major college star who came out of Virginia Tech University as the top overall pick, while Reed was a little-known player chosen in the fourth round. Kelly arrived in 1986 after a successful stint in the short-lived United States Football League, and Thomas joined the Bills in 1988 after a brilliant college career at Oklahoma State University.

Levy built an offensive attack around Kelly, Thomas, and Reed that revolutionized football. Called the "K-gun" offense, it involved Kelly lining up a few yards behind the center in what is called the shotgun formation. From there, Kelly could either hand off or slip a quick pass to Thomas or fire the ball downfield to Reed. The Bills would often run a series of plays without a huddle, not allowing the opposing defense to rest or make substitutions. "Playing against the Bills is like getting caught in a hurricane," said Los Angeles Raiders defensive end Howie Long. "They are relentless."

Andre Reed set virtually every club receiving record^

Like Smith, Pro Bowl linebacker Bryce Paup was a key member of the Bills defense in the 1990s.

On defense, Smith was tireless in his pursuit of
quarterbacks, posting 10 or more sacks per season
in 12 of his 15 years in Buffalo. The exceptionally
quick and powerful end was also a terror against
the run, compelling many opposing offenses to
avoid his side of the line. With Smith wreaking
havoc and his offensive teammates running wild,
the Bills returned to power. "We were blessed to
have a core of guys who gave it everything they
had, every Sunday," said Levy. "It was an honor to
lead such men."

THE POWERFUL BILLS ruled the AFC in the early 1990s. In addition to the great foursome of Kelly, Thomas, Smith, and Reed, Buffalo featured such talented players as receiver Don Beebe and linebacker Cornelius Bennett. Under Coach Levy, the remarkably consistent Bills set an NFL record by reaching four consecutive Super Bowls between 1990 and 1993.

The four-year run began with a 13–3 season in 1990. The Bills then advanced to the AFC championship game, where they crushed the Oakland Raiders 51–3. In the Super Bowl against the New York Giants, the Bills trailed 20–19 with just seconds left in the game. Bills kicker Scott Norwood lined up for a 47-yard field goal that would cap-

Cornelius Bennett used a combination of quickness and cunning to become an expert pass rusher^

Small but hardworking receiver Don Beebe contributed to the Bills' great run in the early '90s

long enough, but it sailed just wide of the uprights, and the Giants won. "That ball slid by that upright by about a foot," Kelly said sadly. "We were a foot away from being champions."

The Bills charged right back to the Super Bowl the next year but lost to the Washington Redskins, 37–24. A year later, Buffalo staged the biggest comeback in NFL playoff history. Down 35–3 to the Houston Oilers, backup quarterback Frank Reich, starting in place of an injured Kelly, fired four touchdown passes in just seven minutes to lead the Bills to an amazing 41–38 victory. The Bills' luck again ran out in the Super Bowl, however, as the Dallas Cowboys cruised to a 52–17 win. A year later, the Bills led the Cowboys 13–6 at halftime in a Super Bowl rematch but ended up losing 30–13.

The great Bills team of the early '90s never made it back to the Super Bowl. Kelly retired after the 1996 season. Levy left the team in 1997, and Thomas, Smith, and Reed all moved on to other teams after the 1999 season. "No matter what the scoreboard said," team owner Ralph Wilson noted, "this team was a champion in my heart."

BUFFALO'S BAD PLAYOFF luck would not change in 1999. After going 11–5 under coach Wade Phillips, the Bills faced the Tennessee Titans in the first round of the playoffs. Late in the game, Steve Christie booted a field goal to give Buffalo a 16–15 lead with just seconds remaining. But on the ensuing kick-off, a Titans blocker handed the ball off to Tennessee tight end Frank Wycheck. Wycheck then fired a long lateral across the field to receiver Kevin Dyson, who sprinted 75 yards down the sideline for the winning score. "My heart sank when I saw that guy cross the goal line," said Bills defensive end Phil Hansen. "I thought the game was in the bag."

At the start of the 21st century, the Bills looked to a new group of stars to return them to glory. Big wide receiver Eric Moulds exploded onto the scene in 2000 by snagging 94 passes. In 2002, running back Travis Henry charged for 1,438 yards on the ground. Opening holes for Henry was 6-foot-6 and 370-pound offensive tackle Mike Williams, another star on the rise.

Receiver Eric Moulds emerged as a Buffalo star with his rare combination of speed and strength

Before the 2002 season, the Bills made a block-
buster trade, acquiring star quarterback Drew
Bledsoe from the New England Patriots. Bledsoe
gave Buffalo an immediate lift, throwing 24 touchdown passes and leading the Bills to an 8–8 record
after a dismal 3–13 season in 2001. Bledsoe, along
with such talented players as hard-hitting linebacker Takeo Spikes and cornerback Nate Clements,
looked to lead Buffalo to better things in 2004 and
beyond. "Drew is one of the top quarterbacks in
the league," said new Bills coach Gregg Williams.
"He is a big part of our winning future."

For more than 40 years, the Buffalo Bills have
provided fans in northwest New York with an end-
less supply of excitement. From their championship days in the AFL to their great run of the '90s,
the Bills have built one of the most loyal fan fol-
lowings in the NFL. With today's Bills on the rise,
it may not be long before a Super Bowl trophy finally makes its way to snowy Buffalo.

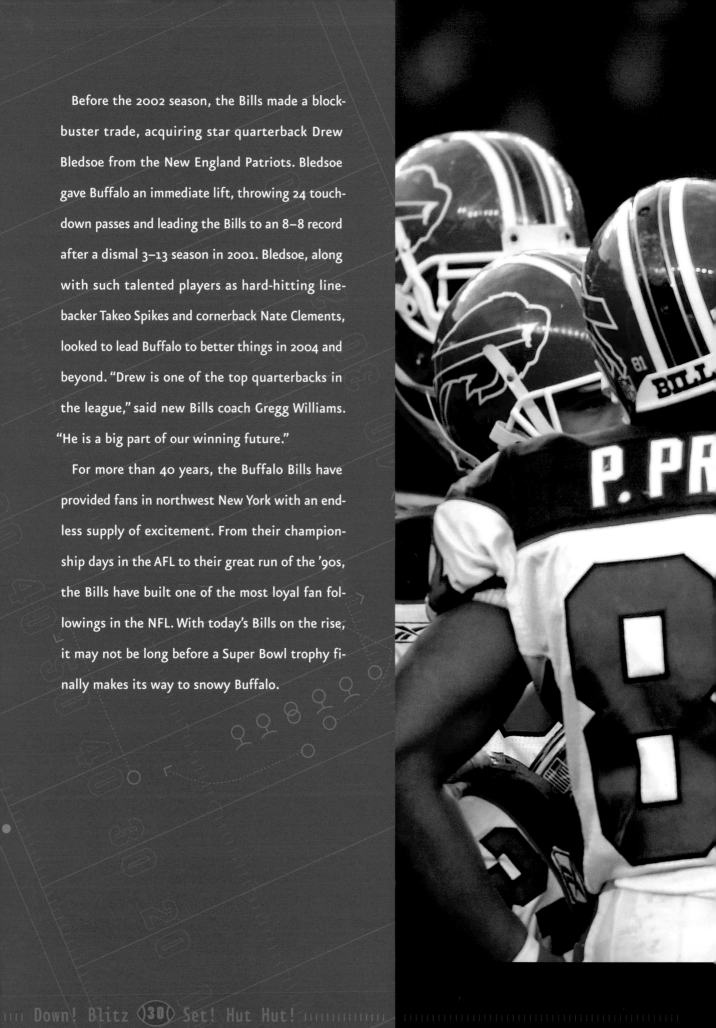

Known for his cool leadership and powerful arm, Drew Bledsoe hoped to lead the Bills back to glory^

INDEX>

The Mouse and

BY BARBARA K. WALKER AND NAKI TEZEL

Parents' Magazine Press • New York

the Elephant

ILLUSTRATED BY EMILY A. McCULLY

Gary Miller

For Alvin Tresselt

Once a small, proud mouse lived in a corner
of the forest. While other mice scurried about,
afraid of their own shadows, he sat idly twirling
his whiskers. From time to time, he stamped upon
the earth and then he put his ear to the ground
and listened. Do you know why? To see whether
the earth trembled!

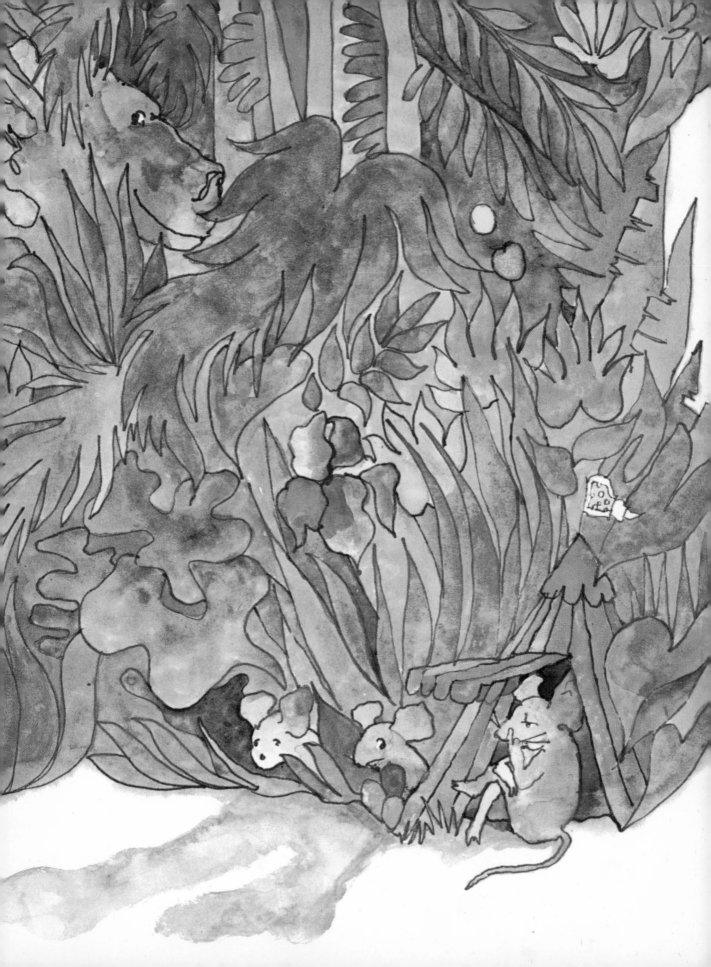

He laughed at the notion that anyone else could be as great and powerful as he was. One day his uncle said wisely, "Watch yourself, young one. The elephant is very angry about your showing off."

"The elephant!" scoffed the little one, who had never seen an elephant. "Who is he? I'll show him who is master of this forest!"

His uncle, old and experienced, smiled behind his paw. "There is something to be said for size. But you must see for yourself, I suppose."

"I shall teach that elephant a lesson," declared the small one. And off he set.

He walked and he walked, till he came upon a
lizard.

"Hey, you," called the mouse. "Are you the
elephant?"

"No, no, not I," answered the lizard. "I am
only a lizard."

"In that case, you may count yourself lucky,"
said the mouse. "If you had been the elephant,
I would have broken you to bits."

The lizard, who had seen the elephant,
shook with laughter. When the mouse heard
the lizard laugh, he stamped his paw with
rage. As it chanced, at that moment there
was a great clap of thunder. The lizard,
thinking the mouse had made all that noise,
scuttled away under a bush.

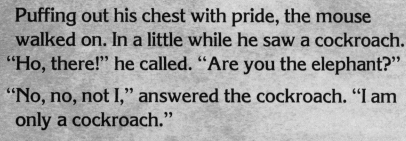

Puffing out his chest with pride, the mouse
walked on. In a little while he saw a cockroach.
"Ho, there!" he called. "Are you the elephant?"

"No, no, not I," answered the cockroach. "I am
only a cockroach."

"In that case, you may count yourself lucky,"
said the mouse. "If you had been the elephant,
I would have broken you to bits."

The cockroach, who had seen the elephant,
shrugged his shoulders. When the mouse saw the
cockroach shrug his shoulders, he glared angrily.
Just as he glared, there came a flash of lightning.

The cockroach, frightened, scurried away.
And the mouse puffed out his chest even more.

He walked on a little farther till he saw a
dog. "How sad he looks," said the mouse to
himself. "It is the elephant, and he must have
heard that I was coming.

"Ho there, elephant!" he called out.

"Elephant!" the dog exclaimed. "I am not the
elephant. I am only a dog." And he smiled
clear across his face.

"Oh, you may safely smile," said the mouse. "But if you had been the elephant, I would have broken you to bits."

Just as the dog was about to answer, a man called to him. "That is my master," said the dog. "For all I know, he is master of the whole world."

"Take that back!" shouted the mouse. "I am master of the whole world."

But the dog had run off, and there was no one to hear.

Still angry, the mouse went on. Suddenly he came
to something that looked as big as a mountain.
It stood on four legs as large as tree trunks.
It had two tails, one in front and one in back.
It had two great ears.

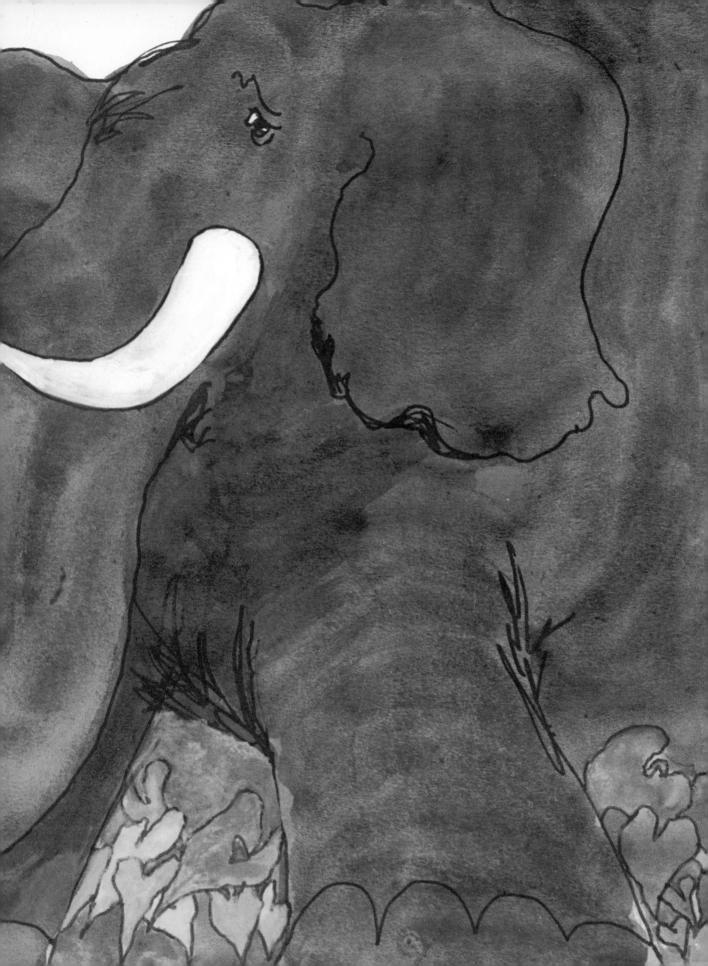

"Hey, you!" called the mouse. "Are you the elephant?"

The elephant looked from bush to tree to rock, and finally he saw a small dot. It was the mouse. He bent his head down so he could hear what the mouse was saying.

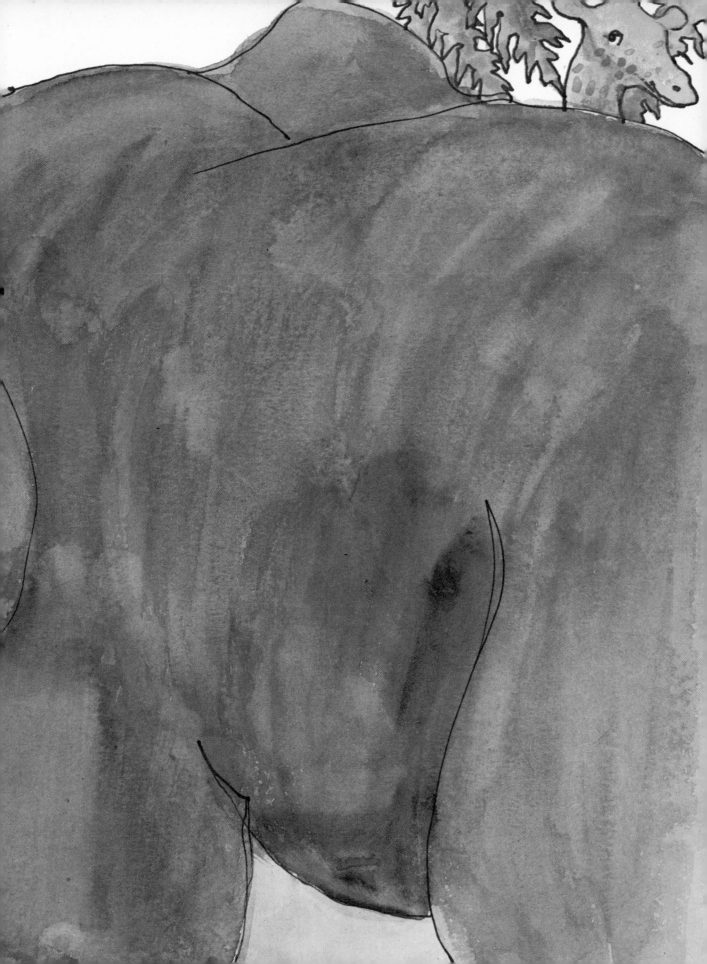

"Who do you think you are?" asked the mouse boldly. "Look at me. I am master of this forest. What do you think of that?"

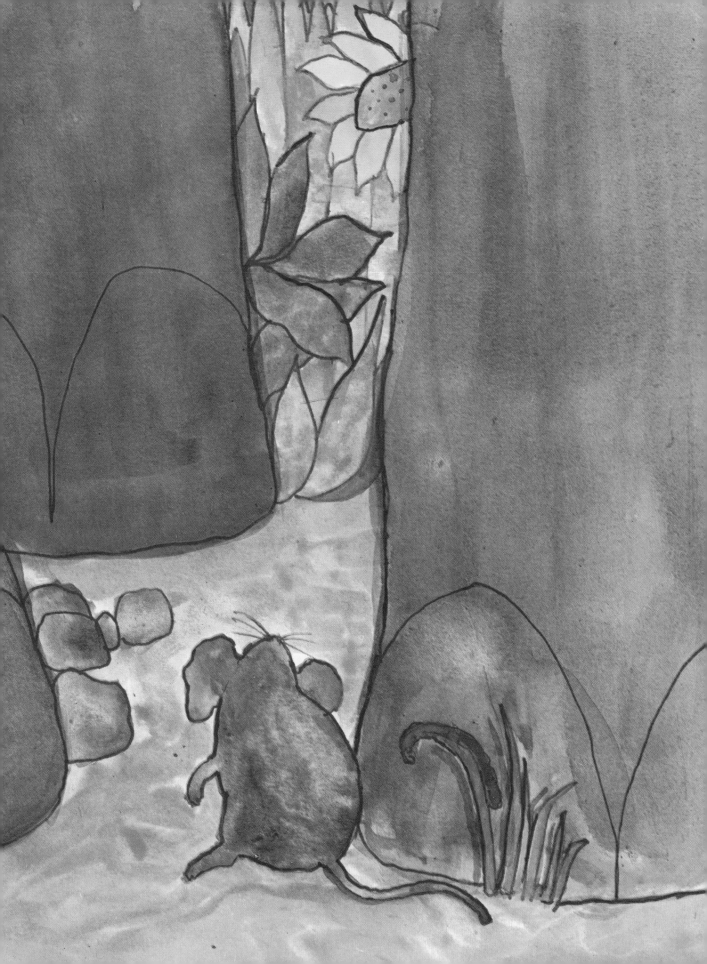

The elephant aimed his trunk at the speck on
the ground and gushed forth all the water he had
sucked up for his bath. Whoosh! The mouse was
thrown heels over ears down the path with the
sudden flood. He lay there for a moment, half-
dead from shock and next-door to drowned, besides.

When he came to his senses again, the elephant
was gone. "What a storm that was!" exclaimed the
mouse. "And it's a lucky thing for that elephant.
If the sky hadn't opened up with a cloudburst, I
would have broken that elephant to bits."

Home he went, walking tall and singing to himself. He smiled clear across his face when he heard the dog barking. "Foolish dog!" he said. "He thinks his man is master of the world. He should have listened to me."

When he saw the cockroach scurry out of the path, he shrugged his shoulders. After all, who could expect a cockroach to know about important matters?

But when he found the lizard hiding under the same bush, he laughed out loud. "I hope you have learned a lesson, my friend," he called. "Next time, take care!"

When he came home, there was his uncle sitting
by the path to greet him. "And did you tell the
elephant who was master of this forest?" asked
his uncle, smiling behind his paw.

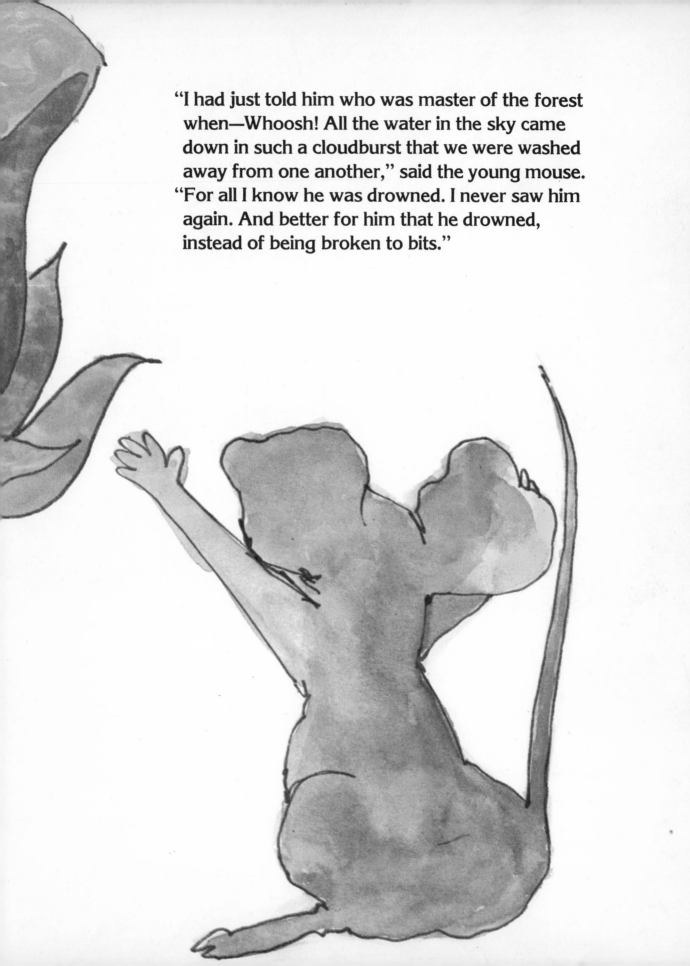

"I had just told him who was master of the forest when—Whoosh! All the water in the sky came down in such a cloudburst that we were washed away from one another," said the young mouse. "For all I know he was drowned. I never saw him again. And better for him that he drowned, instead of being broken to bits."

Down he sat in his old corner. And if the elephant has not come along to dispute him, he is still telling the same story.